NEALE OSBORNE

Jason Rascal's
Autumn
Nightmare

words and pictures, copyright © Neale Osborne, 2015

ISBN: 978-1511963817

This first edition printed by Createspace at Amazon.com

*

titles in the *'Jason Rascal'* series:
'Spring in Time'
'Mad Summer Games'

other available books by Neale Osborne:
'Lydia's Enchanted Toffee'
'Lydia's Golden Drum'

(and for older readers)
'The Castle of Desires'

Jason Rascal's Autumn Nightmare

or

'The
Hallowe'en
Horrors
on
Hexhill
Common'

✝

† Contents †

Contents

† Chapter I †

The Cloak of the Vampire

"I vont to sock yur blod!" said Jason. "You vill look into my eyes! Do as I command! Drive me whe-hair I tell you!"

"Oh *shut up*, Jinx," Felicity winced. (*Jinx* was her nickname for her stepbrother, as she considered him to be her *bad luck charm*.) "Your vampire impression's *rubbish*."

"Not as rubbish as your driving."

"Er, *helloo!* I've got my license now, *thank* you. Anyway, how can I concentrate with *Count Stinkula* sitting next to me?"

Twelve-year-old Jason (who much preferred 'Jase') was off to a Hallowe'en party at his mate's house; his eighteen-year-old stepsister drove him there: Felicity 'Fifi' Fiona Lanky-Snobbington. *Okay, that last bit wasn't her surname - just part of her surly personality.*

She was definitely his wicked stepsister, though; and not 'wicked cool', but rather '*Wicked Witch of the West*'.

The thin wooden man turned to Jase, pumpkin eyes fiery white, the fangy grin growing greater on his face. "The innocent fool removed the charms!" the man rasped, and laughed. "*Ha har!* I'm free of the curse! At last!"

And the scarecrow twirled away, into the tall corn-grass, still laughing hysterically.

Jason stood there, really shaken, hand upon his racing heart. "Oh - okay. That - that was *weird*. But the scarecrow didn't harm me - or try to attack me. So - maybe, I'll be all right, after all." Jase turned to go - "Aay!"

A huge raven stood over him; an ogre of a crow, almost twice his size, with jet black flick-knife wings spread wide.

† Chapter III †

The Blade of the Reaper

The menacing raven leant in nearer, pointing its beak so close to Jase that he nearly gagged at its putrid breath; it smelt as though the bird had eaten stink-bugs for breakfast.

"*Whaat? Whaat?*" the raven aasked. "Whaat sort o' scrawny insect, are *you?*" And the crow poke-poked Jase's shoulder with one of its sharp-edged feathers.

"Ow!" Jase winced, as the feather almost cut him.

"Trespaassin' on my croperty, ya thievin' little baasket!"

"I - I'm not a thief!" Jase replied, hoping that the raven hadn't seen him take the bracelet.

"I'll snip off your fingers, if ya don't git out of 'ere faast!" And the black bird swished its blade-filled wings.

Jase was more than happy to oblige, and was just about to go, when he heard the crow cry out in alarm:

"Whaat in hellfire happened to my scare-fella?"

"He - he came to life," said Jase. "And ran away."

"Raak! Raak! Raak!" the bird squawked in distress, madly slashing its feathers at the blood-suckers, cutting some of them up, severing wings, before falling to the ground, wholly overwhelmed by the bat-like things.

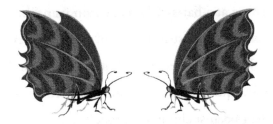

Jase scrambled to his feet, and sprinted away. He ran and ran through the tall corn-grass, till he found he was in a different field. The boy stopped. He twitched his nose.

"Urh," he sniffed. "Something's burning!"

Jase now tramped through a field filled with hundreds upon hundreds of head-high stalks ~ thick, splintery wooden stems with weird bulbous pink growths on the ends.

'They're gigantic matchsticks!' he realized, proceeding with caution as the burning niff grew ever more pungent.

Since leaving the raven, Jase also kept hearing these bursts of chirpy trilling chirrs; and now, as he squeezed his way past the matchsticks, the noises were louder and all around him: a twittery cricketty chirruping chitchat.

Jason chanced upon more massive creatures, insects this time, smaller than the raven, though taller than himself. A crowd of them emerged from the matchsticks to surround him.

'*Urh!*' Jase shuddered, as the creatures looked really gross, up close: their palpy mouthparts, blank brown eyes, flickering feelers, and quick stick-thin limbs (six of them, naturally), two being larger back legs, while four were forelimbs, armed with claws.

These particular beasts were brown-bodied crickets (marked with bold golden bands), and they ganged up on Jase, jostling and pushing him, digging him in the back with their feelers and claws.

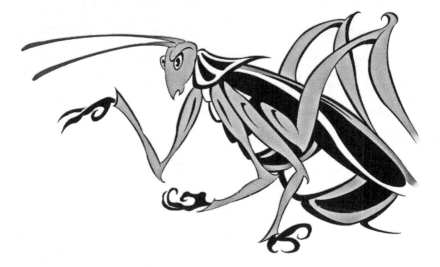

"Who d'you support?" the insects pestered him, sounding like a load of soccer hooligans. "Who d'you think's best? Crickets or grasshoppers? Brilliant crickets or crappy grasshoppers?"

"*Er-*" Jase took a wild guess. *"Crickets?"*

"He looks like a stinking grasser fanatic to me!" chirred one.

"No," Jase answered. "Crickets are best! Honest!"

"D'you like *Bounders* then? We just off to a match!"

"The chap can be our lucky mascot," chirruped another.

"Yes! You can sit with our team and watch."

"Er, o - kay," uttered Jase uneasily, worried that, if he disagreed, the intimidating insects would duff him up.

The mob of crickets shoved him along through the field of matches and, before long, they reached a scorched-away clearing, a circular area covered with soot, a pitch around which masses more insects had gathered: half of them were crickets coloured brown-and-yellow, while the rest were grasshoppers, steely green, slightly bigger with shorter antennae.

† Chapter IV †

The Clash of the Giant Grasshoppers

The afternoon light was fading now, so the crickets lit a load of the match-stalks, striking them till they sparked into life, then sticking them around the edge of the pitch as flickering fiery floodlights. Their eerie orange radiance shone across the masses of insect spectators, and snakes of grey sulphurous smoke twisted in the air above the creepy scene.

Jase guessed that some strange game was about to take place on the ashen pitch ~ a game of territorial rivalry between the two species: field crickets versus grasshoppers; throngs of them in opposition, jeering, chanting, stridulating, stamping legs and rasping wings to make a massed cacophonous buzz.

A grand wooden 'bread bin' pavilion had been built at the grasshoppers' side of the pitch; whereas the crickets had a crummy cardboard dugout (a giant matchbox half in the ground).

This was where the gang of insects took Jase, to present him to their team. The dugout was lined with scratchy sandpaper, and "Ow!" Jase painfully grazed his elbow, as the crickets chucked him in, and left him there to watch.

The game looked like regular 'cricket' on the face of it, with two sets of corn-stalk stumps (or wickets) set up at the centre of the soot-covered pitch; between the stumps was a flour-sprinkled strip, at the ends of which were two round plates. *('Okay,'* thought Jase, *'that's a bit unusual.'* But then he remembered that this game was called *Bounders* and was bound to differ from the sport he knew.)

"Lucky mascot! Lucky mascot!" the superstitious crickets cheered as they went to take the field, each punching the boy in the arm, or clipping him round his head 'for luck'. Jase counted thirteen crickets in brown-and-gold colours (that meant thirteen flippin' thumps); and the spindly-legged 'fielders' were soon joined by a pair of grasshopper 'batters' in the middle of the match-lit pitch.

One cricket remained in the dugout: the non-playing captain; bigger and meaner than the rest of the team, it bossed them about - and Jason too, pushing him, making him stand up straight, expecting him to take a morbid interest in this insect grudge-match.

"Right, *nymph*," he chirruped at the boy, "as you've never even seen Bounders before, I'm going to explain the game. One team fields - that's *us* first - while the other team bats - that's the *rubbish* grasshoppers. Now, our doler bowls three balls of dough to hit the wickets; this is termed a tray delivery and, after four trays or a dozen doughs, the doler's done an oven full, so another has a go. The batters come in to bake two-at-a-time, the game's aim to score as many from an oven while protecting the wicket by batting the doled dough balls and bounding round the boundary, thus baking a bun. When one baker claims thirteen concurrent buns, that is a baker's dozen and so the batter has a break, to let the next batter bake."

Jason nodded, not understanding a thing.

"Now you know the ins 'n' outs," the captain continued. "it's best you be acquainted with the possible shots: a batter can cut the dough, slog it, swipe it, slice it, dice it, drive it, hook it, pull it or sweep. But a batter-baker mustn't be baled, bowled or bound out, or snick their own wicket, clip the dole to a waiter, or kick it. Do these thrice and they must quickly quit the pitch. When there are no more bakers to deliver trays of dough to, the innings has fizzled, and the batter team takes a turn to dole dough.

And *vicey-verso*. Now to summarize: it's a batter baker, jump a bound, a bound a bun, a bun a run, a dole a ball, a ball o' dough, a dozen doughs and the oven is over."

"Will this game take long?" grumbled Jase, recalling that some cricket games lasted for days!

But the captain ignored him, as play had begun, and the insects in the field were already doling dough balls to the grasshopper batter there at the plate.

Jase could now see that the bats being used were real live bats with leathery wings, and the many-limbed insects were able to wield three at once (which was just as well, as the dolers bowled three balls of dough at once too). When a wacky bat's swinging wings whacked a ball, the baker who batted it became a 'bounder', leaping laps around the boundary, in order to run a bun for the team.

In the outer pitch, though, were the cricket 'waiters', those waiting for the dough to come their way, collecting and returning the balls to the doler, who then leapt between the sets of wickets to deliver it to the other baker at the other end. And so the whole business of delivering 'trays of dough' began again in a loopy loop. Jase was glad he was simply a spectator; this game just as utterly batty as the rules.

The cricketty critters sprang about, catching, throwing, bowling, doling; half-a-dozen dough balls whistled through the air, with half-a-dozen flapping bat wings whacking them; grasshopper-batters jumped umpteen feet fast, rounding the boundary, kicking up ashes, and running up buns. When one grasshopper was 'out' three times (when a dough ball hit its leg or the wicket, or was caught, without bouncing, off the bat by a cricket) then it had to take a bake-off and hop it to the bread bin; the game barely paused while the next grasshopper batter bounded to the middle.

Despite what the mean cricket captain had said, though, the rival green team wasn't rubbish at all; and standing in the matchbox dugout, Jason watched the pairs of grasshoppers slogging and pounding the dough balls in every direction, running the crickets ragged round the pitch, and whipping up a record-breaking batch of buns.

Eventually, however, as the last grasshopper took its break (having scored a baker's dozen without being out), the innings was over, and the teams called 'tea-time'. This first half of the match was done-and-dusted in just a few manic minutes. *'Phew!'* thought Jase, relieved. *'At least this game won't last much longer!'*

The whacked-out cricket team met in the dugout, and the captain all but bit their heads off. "We've never bin beaten this badly before!" it chirped. "Now get out there and clobber those grasshoppers! Slaughter 'em! Smash 'em round the park! Or else!"

So the crickets took their turn to go and bat-a-bake. And, as before, they each gave Jase a quick punch in the arm or clip round the ear (out of spite, this time, instead of superstition - as the boy hadn't been *at all* lucky for them.)

However, the match was soon over; the grasshoppers proved to be skillful dolers, serving up fastballs, curveballs, sour-doughs and spinning googlies bamboozling the batters. The crickets lost quick wickets ~ bowled out, baled out, found out, bound out, caught out and taken out when three times over done.

Jase edged away from the irate captain who leapt up and down in the sandpaper dugout, kicking up sparks, spitting up grass, ranting and raving, and ticking off his team:

"No! No! What a scrappy shot! Utterly lacking in batting technique! You're giving your wicket away! Wicket away! Wicket away! Stupid stumpid skipping crickets! We're losing! Losing! Getting thrashed and roasted! Absolutely battered and buttered and toasted!"

The captain may have been fuming furious ~ but that was nothing compared to the insect spectators who chirruped angrily, grylling out insults:

"Jammy bounder! Dirty grasser! Stinking cricket!" and other distinctly *un-sportsmanlike* names.

Portions of the disgruntled crowd began to throw lighted firecrackers too. So, as the batters leapt off the pitch ~ *Cracker bang bang!* ~ they were hit by mini missiles.

Another cricket went in to bake, but came back bunless. *Cracker bang smack!* Another in. Another out. *Smacker cracker bang!* It all happened so fast.

"Out! Out! Out!" the grasshoppers cried as dough balls clattered into legs and stumps; wickets went skittling; bakers with flappy bats were hit by flashing fireworks.

And so it was, the innings fizzled, ending in a most humiliating defeat with every cricket over and out. The grasshoppers had trounced them, and their victory taunts triggered all-out war between the swarms of supporters. Around the ground there was a vicious clash of insects, a pitched battle with more flaring fireworks thrown across the field. Violent scuffles broke out amongst the players too, and with all the fighting, the stridulant screeching and crackling explosions, Jason tried to sneak away ~

However, the cricket captain noticed: "Lucky mascot?" scowled the insect. "*Bad luck jinx!* You cost us the match!"

"Yes!" bristled the rest of the team. "*Jinx! Jinx! He's* why we lost! Let's flog him and slog him! Then throw him on a grill!" they trilled.

"Yes, let's punish him!" the captain kept on. "Cut him up! De-caput-hate him! Make him our trophy! Chip his head off!"

And while the insects bickered and snickered, devising the best most horrendous vengeance, Jase decided to make a break for it. He scrammed from the dugout, and nipped into the field (avoiding the hotspots of match-lit fighting), hoping to lose the crickets in the thicket. His progress was aimless, arm-flailing frustration, splintery stalks tearing at his cloak. Jason feared that the giant insects, with their leaping capabilities, would catch him in no time ~ then kill him and grill him and eat him for tea.

The boy dashed on and on, batting his hands through the mass of matches, on and on, till everything was quieter.

Jason paused to take a breath, almost sure the danger had passed. He took a hold of the unlucky bracelet, and was just about to throw it away, when he saw the wheat-like trinket glow and disappear ~

Suddenly ~ *Crash! Clash!* A bombardment of bodies thudded down behind him as the squad of crickets dive-bombed the field. Dead scared, Jase cowered on the ground as the barrage of creatures crash-landed around him, screeching their high-pitched shrillipy cries.

Feu! Feu-feu! There were flashes of flame where friction had sparked off the tops of the match-stalks, and Jason saw all his attackers transfixed on them, their thoraxes run through, pierced by the sulphurous spears, spitten on the flaming stakes, like specimen insects in a collector's display case. Jase fled, horrified, leaving the crickets screaming, writhing, fried alive like shish kebabs. He ran and ran till he left the field of matches and its stench of roasting insect flesh.

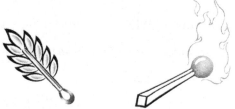

Next, he stumbled upon a pasture where the wood-splint grass had been scythed to stubble and heaped into stacks, their spiky silhouettes visible in the moonlight.

During the course of the cricket conflict, the sky had blackened over to night.

The only sounds Jase now heard were slow echoey *clips* and *clops*, the creaking cranking of heavy wooden wheels, and ~ *lash! lash!* ~ intermittent *smacks* of a whip.

Hiding beside a splintery stack, he spied on this approaching vehicle: a colossal wagon, being driven by a raven, and pulled by a ginormous aphid bug!

Jase was tired from all his running; still, he felt he should keep on the move, so he snuck up behind the trundling wagon, jumped to the back, gripped onto a timber, and managed to awkwardly clamber aboard.

Another vast stack of matchsticks was stuck on the back of the raven's wagon; it towered over Jase, as big as a cottage and, as he tiptoed his way around it, he heard these whispery voices close by. The boy didn't dare move; the murmurs were intelligible yet, similar to the crickets' chirrups, they sounded somewhat *inhuman* to his ears.

'More giant pests, no doubt.'

Jason didn't dare take a look either, so he lay there, weary, against the stick-stack, staying as quiet as he could.

One of the unidentified creatures was about to tell a Hallowe'en story, and Jase heard the words as pictures in his mind, dreamlike images, lurid and gory …

† Chapter V †

The Tale of the Blazing Man

Once there was, in the county of Arachnashire, a stinking rich spider by the name of Money-Spinner who owned many farms across the countryside.

A horde of harvestmen tended to his territory: his cereal fields, caterpillar pastures, orchards, and herds of cattle-flies. Yet every year, these workers were paid a measly pittance for all their toil, while the avaricious Money-Spinner sat there in his mansion (a luxury dwelling with dozens of web-rooms) wallowing in his filthy wealth.

Come Fall, his fields would be flush with lush golden wheat; the orchards swollen full of sweet-fleshed fruit; the herds of caterpillars lumpy plump; and the cattle-flies fattened up for flogging at the market.

This was Money-Spinner's favourite season when his dirty great profits piled high like horsefly manure.

And so it was, one Autumn time, the harvestmen who worked his land asked for a raise. The thought of the wages of these loathsome labourers eating into his precious income always made the landowner sick.

"That scrounging rabble!" Money-Spinner seethed to a colleague called Money-Grubber (also a rich, bloated spider who owned whole tracts of Arachnashire). "Those harvestmen know that we have no choice but to meet their demands: the fields need reaping, the fruits need collecting, the caterpillars and cattle-flies need slaughtering for meat."

Money-Grubber faced a similar predicament. "Aye! And if we give in to that riff-raff, they'll ask us for more and more each year!"

"They'll bleed us dry, the bleeding ticks!" Money-Spinner feared. "If only we could find someone else to do the work instead – for half the pay!"

"Or for free!" sniggered Grubber.

"For free," grinned Spinner. "Aah, that would be magic!"

"Magic, you say?" Grubber had an idea. "In the town of Herbfest live three old widows. It is said they are witches versed in black magic. Maybe they can help us in our hour of desperation."

"A curse on the workers!" Money-Spinner toasted, guzzling a vintage fly-blood wine. "Let us go see these witches – this minute!"

Later that night, the two tipsy money-spiders took their horsefly-driven coach to Herbfest.

It was a foul, wet night, a lightning storm lighting up the rain-lashed lanes, as they made their way to a ramshackle shack in a run-down part of town. This hovel was home to the three widow crones; eerie green light flickered from a window, and Spinner and Grubber approached the shack, knock-knock-knocking thrice upon its rotting door.

They waited there, in mounting trepidation, shivering in the stinging rain until, at last –

Creeak!

The mouldering door groaned slowly open and, in the dim candlelight, they beheld three frail spiders wrapped in thin web-white shawls. The trio of sisters (Black, Red, and Brown Widow) invited Spinner and Grubber inside; and there in the cobweb-cosy hovel they sat around a cooking pot where a luminous slime green soup bubbled hot, chunky with hunks of blackened fly; here a marinated leg, there a proboscis, and – blup! – a bobbing compound eye.

Money-Spinner explained their dilemma.

"If you help us," he told the old widows, "we could spare a penny or three for your pains."

"Oh, we do not want your money," said Red.

"Our services," added Black with a cackle, "will only cost you an arm and a leg!"

"Two tasty limbs from you, Money-Spinner," said Brown. "And two from you, Money-Grubber!"

The witchy widows chuckled peckishly.

"You promise," the half-sozzled Money-Spinner whimpered, "that your magic will save us lots of precious money?"

"We swear on our husbands' graves," vowed the widows.

And so, most reluctantly, the two money-spiders agreed.

Black Widow fetched her sharpest fruit-fly-knife.

Chop chop! *Scream! Scream!* Blup-lup! *went the soup.*

Mmm. *The witches ate well, that night.*

The very next morn, on All Hallows' Eve, the widows went to their cemetery garden. There they assembled a wooden skeleton: its limbs from the timber of a hangman's gallows (with fingers and toes of rusted nails); its spine the handle from a gravedigger's spade; its head the wheel of a shipwrecked ship; all tied together with their very own silk.

That evening, Spinner and Grubber returned (each now missing an arm and a leg) to see the skeleton standing in the graveyard garden. The trio of widows recited a spell, and the skeletal man - Creeak! - came to life. And, before their eyes, it grew in size to three four five times the spiders' height.

"Wicca Man!" Black Widow called to the giant. "Go with these two money-spiders and undertake any work they require."

And the wooden man nodded his wheel-shaped head, and plodded after the spiders' coach, across the county to their fields and farms.

39

"Let us set the Wicca Man to work right away," said Spinner. And he issued a command to the great wooden skeleton, and watched it take a scythe in each hand, and lumber away into the moonlit pastures.

By morning, all the wheat was reaped and stacked to the utter delight of the greedy landowners.

As the days passed, the Wicca Man toiled on without food or rest, doing the work of scores of harvestmen, tirelessly labouring, never complaining or claiming wages. And so Money-Spinner and Money-Grubber were able to dispose of half their workforce ~ taking particular pleasure in firing those who had asked for more pay.

"Get off my land, you bleedin' parasites!" Spinner spat as he gave them the axe. "Ha ha! Chop chop! And don't come back!"

Many of the harvestmen became enraged, watching the Wicca Man, day after day, reaping and heaping without any pay, stealing their livelihoods away.

40

So, one night, while the wooden giant toiled, one ex-worker took a torch, sneaked into the wheat field, and set fire to the skeleton's legs. Whoosh! *The Wicca Man lit up in a burst of flame, staggering on, its timber limbs ablaze, till ~* Crreeak!

The giant toppled ~ Crrunch! ~ *smashing into pieces as it hit the ground, crackling to ashes, and crumbling lifeless into the earth. The countryside fell deathly silent.*

The wooden figure was seen no more.

†

The next morn, Spinner and Grubber limped across the half-reaped field, puzzling over the ashen remains.

"Where the hell's our Wicca Man gone?" they asked. "We gave up an arm and a leg for nothing!"

Suddenly, however ~ Spit Spat Sputter! ~ *the ashes sparked into fiery life. The money-spiders cowered, scared, as a sprightly demon grew from the soil.*

It was the spirit of the enchanted skeleton, released from his spell of eternal toil; and now he rose, a Blazing Man of terrifying fire, with a wheel of whirling flame for a head.

Money-Grubber froze in fear as the demon reached out with a crackling hand and closed five fiery fingers around him. The Blazing Man burned Grubber to a crisp and tossed his crooked blackened corpse across the field ~ Crrunch!

Money-Spinner screamed in terror, and scurried off as quickly as his loppy legs would carry him.

And so the Blazing Man moved on, leaving a trail of death and devastation; fields became roaring pastures of flame; the fruit in the orchards charred on the trees; the lumpy plump caterpillars shrivelled up at the fiery man's touch; and the cattle-flies were roasted alive, left as worthless herds of deadstock. Money-Spinner was soon made penniless, all of his earthly riches going up in smoke.

And still the Blazing Man went on ~ from field to field, farm to farm, from county town to county town ~ a relentless monstrous force of nature, an elemental man created by witchcraft. Wherever he stepped, fire raged, consuming fields and crops and trees; spreading his blazey disease across the country, leaving no barn, no home unburned. Plumes of smoke smothered the land.

The man could be seen for miles around, blazing fearsomely, beacon bright, against the darkened smoky sky, grown to epic epidemic proportions.

The population tried desperately to stop him; setting elaborate spiderweb snares, building fences, digging moats, diverting rivers in a bid to contain him. But the Blazing Man leapt the obstacles with ease, and burned right through the fences and snares.

The spineless Money-Spinner blamed the widows of Herbfest town, and an angry pack of wolf spiders dragged them from their shack, and forced the three witches to confront the fiery giant.

"Wicca Man!" cried the frail old crones. "We created you! You must obey! Now cease your terrible destruction this day!"

Hearing the widows' pleading calls, the Blazing Man came to a sudden halt. Then he turned, and stamp-stamp-stamped the witches flat, leaving three cremated splats. The town spiders looked on, shocked, as the Blazing Man moved off once more. It seemed that the giant could not be stopped.

Many wicked weeks passed. The Blazing Man travelled the countryside, laying waste to the web-patterned land.

Then one day, in the black smoke sky, a single cloud drifted by. A single snowflake fell upon Arachnashire - a flake that made the Blazing Man shake, quiver and shiver as it sizzled against him. Soon, across the ruined landscape, sleet beat down; then thickening snowflakes, a blistering blizzard that smothered the Blazing Man, dowsing his body, his head and limbs, and - with a fizzle of flame, and a hiss of smoke - the fire fellow died. And the Blazing Man was never seen again.

So to this day, at Autumn's end, once the harvest is safely away, the spiders celebrate, and pay their respects to the power of nature ~ making bonfire offerings of hay on which they burn replica wicker men. "Bon Fire! Good Fire!" they cry, and shoot warning rockets into the sky. Because the arachnids ever fear that, at any time, the Blazing Man will rise ...

Har ha-ha ha-ha har!

At the chilling tale's conclusion, the narrator laughed harshly, jolting Jason back to his nightmare.

The boy's sudden movements made a crackling noise.

"Whassat? Who's 'ere?" came these creatures' hushed voices. "There's summuz spyin' on us! Gah, let's get 'im!"

Jase tried to scramble away over the wood stack, but he lost his footing, put his hands out to break his fall ~

"Ooo!" the sticks stabbed into his palms. "Ow!" A splinter pierced his skin. Jase had to tweezer it out with his fingers. "Ow ee oh oo ee," he winced.

As he sat there helpless, two figures loomed above him; their claws wrenched him to his feet, and Jase stood facing a pair of stag beetles, bulky black insects with antler-like jaws (plus weird white markings down their fronts, so it looked as though they were wearing tuxedos).

45

One of the beetles noticed Jason's injured palm.

"Did ya bodge yourself?" it asked. "Let's see." And it snatched at his wrist, and sucked some blood from his hand before the boy could pull it away.

"*Urh*," Jase squirmed.

"Mmm'z a tasty drop o' blood." The beetle clacked its jaws for approval. "Tell ya what - We'll let ya in the club."

"Club?" said Jase.

"Yeah, *club*. 'Ere, have a *butchers*." Using their pincers, the pair of beetles parted some larger sticks in the stack; Jason saw a light within, like the embers of a bonfire. "Quick-wick, get in, before summuz sees ya."

Jase was hesitant about entering the stack, but the insects pushed him in and bustled up behind, and he found himself inside the most unlikely hideaway.

† Chapter VI †

The Deadly Den of Abominable Beetles

Within the wood stack, Jase discovered a den of sorts, dimly-lit with jam jar lanterns (luminescent fireflies trapped inside); the whole place swayed with the motion of the wagon, its arched walls of interwoven tinder sticks crackling and creaking precariously around him, as if they could all fall apart at any moment.

More humungous stag beetles (in shiny black tuxedo shells) stood at wheel-shaped tables, drinking; some were even smoking cigars (with a distinctive stink of rolled-up dung.)

Jase was greeted by a ladybird hostess:

"Welcome to the Bonfire Nightclub," she cheeped, and showed him and his beetle companions to a table.

One of the stags had a bag of chips, slices of potato which were used to buy a round of drinks.

At a nearby bar, the insects' refreshments were served from a row of coppery pots; ladybirds ladled out soup into bowls (which were more like colanders, riddled with holes so they dripped and dribbled everywhere). The jolting of the raven's wagon didn't help either, and a sickly slick of snotty broth slopped back 'n' forth across the floor. The beetles didn't mind though; holding the bowls up in their jaws, they sucked the yucky leaky soup.

The ladybird barmaid chirped as she poured:

"Colander soup, dribble dribble, colanders bleed.

Hold up your cups to the ladle. Lick your bowls clean."

Other lady-bug waitresses circulated, passing round pint-sized acorn cups, pocketing the customers' chips and tips. The stag beetles slurped down the beery beverages, fermented fruit juices, and slugs of bitter aphid blood.

"Beer Beer. Black berry. Have another drink?

Here, here, thank ee, sirs," the ladybirds did wink.

The den was also part-casino, and many of the denizens were engaged in various games of chance (and, in some cases, *of life or death*).

Jase decided to look around and, at one of the tables, he saw two beetles paying a weevil a few tasty crisps, before entrusting whole packets of potato chips to it.

The weevil then placed a pair of identical mushrooms in front of them.

"Oo, what are you playing?" Jason asked.

"M-Mushroom Roulette," stammered one of the participants.

"Do you want to sit in or not?' the weevil snorted through its snout.

"I - *er*, I'll just watch." Jase didn't have any money anyway. "So how do you play?"

"One - one of the funguses is d-deadly poisonous," said the nervous beetle. "While the other m-mushroom is harmless. But we don't know which."

"Now, gentle-beetles, place your bites," urged the weevil.

Jase looked on as the pair of beetles scoffed their respective mushrooms down.

Then there came a sombre silence, a heartstopping wait ~ before the beetle that had eaten the poisonous mushroom started to shake; its legs waggled frantically till ~ *Clunk!* ~ it flipped on its back, and snuffed it.

The beetle left alive was then given all the dead one's chips; and the weevil moved the still-quivering corpse, and invited two more insects to risk their lives in this grisliest of games. *'Ugh, I'm not staying here,'* thought Jase, and quickly looked elsewhere.

At the next table, three female leaf beetles (wearing what seemed to be sequinned dresses) sat before handfuls of twigs and straw, using them to make poppet dolls, to the rolls of a six-sided dice. This intrigued Jase as he had once played a similar game called *'Beetle Drive'*; yet instead of assembling plastic bugs, the insects were twisting together little wicker men, adding parts, one at a time, depending on the number on the dice:

It was '1' for an upper body; '2' for a tummy; '3' for a head; '4' for the legs; '5' for the arms; and at the roll of a '6', the beetles added matchstick antennae, little twiggy feelers sticking from the stick-man's head. (Jase also noticed that the beetles gave the poppet people *four* arms, as well.)

"One!" they cried, and made a little wicker thorax - onto which "Four five!" they started to plonk on the limbs.

"Three!" called one. "A head for me."

"Oo, six!" said another, and added a matchstick.

"This one's done!" cried the third leaf beetle, and shoved it in Jase's face. "Har, little dolly boy! It looks like you!"

"Har ha-har!" The others laughed. "What an ugly pugly buggyman! Look at his preposterous proportions. Fatty legs and poky eyes!"

"His portions look normal to me," said Jase. "Well, apart from his *extra* parts. Look, you don't make people like that!"

"Oh shut your yap!" the beetles snapped. "Go away! To blazes with ya!" And they carried on throwing the dice to make the wicker men - and, when complete, (or, in Jase's opinion *completely wrong*) they set the dolls on fire by striking the antennae matches. "Six! Six! Light the sticks! *Har ha-har!* Watch the silly dolly burn!"

'I'd better get out of here,' thought Jase. *'Stupid beetles playing with fire - especially in a stack of sticks!'*

The den continued to tremble unsteadily, as the wagon rumbled along. In one corner of the club, an audience of stag beetles revelled in a macabre cabaret.

By the flickering light of the firefly lanterns, a 'glamorous' scarlet ladybird sang. (The songs sort of sounded familiar to Jase ~ yet, like everything else in this place, they were twisted, distorted 'cursery rhymes').

"Three blinded mites. See how they stumble,
Blundering into the farmer's knife.
The blade did slice off their heads in a trice;
their carrion carried on screaming with life.
You've never seen such a hilarious sight
as those three blinded mites."

Clap clap!

"Hinta-spalinter, beetle. Swinging from the gallow tree.

Down you cut, and dead you put –

Zhupsz! – Onto the fire go ye!"

"Sing a song of insects, a thicket full of grit.

Gored intesty black bugs sizzling on a spit.

With their elytra opened, the bugs began to stink.

They made a raven's tasty dish of jaws and claws and wings."

Clap clap!

"Whoooh, it's funny cuz it's true," the listeners muttered, sitting there all jittery, as the ladybird crooned her gruesome tunes.

Jase now nosed around the far side of the wooden den (hoping to find an exit there). He stood by a table, behind a black-and-white-striped Colorado beetle who dished out potatoes as if they were cards; most were plain ones, cut in half, and burnt with numbers (one to six), but other spuds had higher values: jacket potatoes or *King Edwards* (marked 'J' and 'K' respectively.)

The Colorado beetle jumbled up the half-potatoes in a basket under the table, placing four at random in these little cloth sacks. *"One potato, two potato, three potato, four."* And he passed these to the punters in exchange for chips (while keeping one sack for himself, as the 'house dealer.') There were three stag beetle gamblers hunched around the table, drinking liquor, smoking cigars, and playing this particular game of *Spud Poker*.

"Gentle-beetles," the Colorado dealer ordered, "unfold your bags. Let us see what fate has dealt you."

The beetles took furtive peeks inside their mini sacks of spuds, and bet their chips before revealing the contents.

Amidst the dingy shadows, and dungy cigar smoke, Jason noticed the crafty Colorado switch his sack with one under the table, taking advantage of the drunken gamblers dulled by their heady bloody beverages.

The striped dealer-beetle opened this bag to reveal four potatoes each marked with a letter K. "House wins again!" the Colorado declared, and raked up all the players' chips.

"Four kings! A royal mash!" the gamblers groaned. "Oh what are the odds?"

"I had a pair of jack-jacket potatoes too!" moaned one of the stags.

"I had all sixes!" grumbled another. "I wuz sure I'd won!"

The third beetle, who'd bet and lost everything, caught a glimpse of Jase: "Is him! That jinx!" the insect pointed. "Brought me nought but bad bug's luck!"

"Yes!" added a ladybird. "You'd only lost half your chips before *he* arrived."

"Aye!" exclaimed the second stag. "I was merely broke, but now I'm bankrupt! I don't own two balls of dung to rub together!"

"I've been ruined too!" claimed his neighbour. "I'm bloody well skint! Had me chips!"

"Tain't my fault!" protested Jase. "You've all been cheated by a crooked dealer!"

"*Crooked?*" fumed the Colorado. "*Cheaters*, are we? How dare you! That's slander!"

"Chuck the liar on a fire!" cried the ladybird.

A burly goliath beetle bouncer was called.

"Grab that bounder!" shouted the dealer. "Beat him up and chuck him out!"

A crowd of angry bugs surrounded Jase, their mandibles snap-snapping at him. One of them grasped the boy with its claws, another took a cigar and prodded a smouldering hole in Jase's waistcoat.

The Colorado beetle even picked his pocket ~ and held up the charm bracelet. All the insects looked on in alarm.

"Aah!" they cried. "The Pumpkin King's curse!"

"No wonder you was all wiped out!" the Colorado dealer lied. "It was *blackest magic* what made them four kings appear!"

"Yes!" a gambler beetle shouted. "Cleaned me out! Four kings! Four kings!"

Suddenly though ~

"I'll clean you out!" The loud squawk of a crow was heard. *"I'll clean you out! I'll give you forkings!"*

And the prongs of a huge pitchfork came ploughing through the nightclub wall, spearing the dealer right through the abdomen, the stabbed beetle struggling in agony.

Next, there was uproar.

Tables were upturned; spuds and mushrooms flew around the room, leaky soup bowls, fluttering fireflies (freed from their lantern jars) filled the air.

"A raid! A raid!" the beetles cried. "Bale out!"

The farmer raven continued to poke his fork around the den and, in the commotion, Jase nabbed back the bracelet. He saw the 'candle charm' glow and vanish from the chain. Then a fire began to spread through the nightclub.

'It couldn't be a coincidence,' he figured. *'The bracelet must be able to conjure up some wicked magic - especially when I'm in a pickle of a panic!'*

Jase made sure he stayed well away from the pitchfork hacking at the walls of the wood stack; and, as he peered from the half-demolished den he saw a whole mob of ogre ravens approaching. *'Raak! Raak! Raak!'* their scary cries.

Jase had to risk jumping off the wagon; he leapt to the stony ground ~ "Ow!" He hurt his knee as he tumbled, but managed to scamper-limp into the tall grass without being spotted by the murderous birds.

With a feverish rattling, the weevils, beetles, and squealing ladybirds were driven from the splintery den. The *Bonfire Nightclub* was certainly living up to its name, the whole place now a roaring inferno.

Outside the stack, the insects were ambushed by the farmer crows, who cut them down with scything feathers, or jabbed them up with sharpened forks. Some beetles tried to unfold their elytra, open their wings and fly away. But ~ *'Raak! Raak!' Poke! Slash!* ~ those not slaughtered by the ravens, perished in the flaming stack.

With all that kerfuffle (the killing and screaming, and roaring fire), the giant aphid, that was tethered to the wagon, suddenly bolted, and Jason watched the fiery vehicle rumble away, with a pack of squawking raven reapers flapping after, giving chase.

† Chapter VII †

The Coven of Hocus-Pocus Spiders

Jase now cut across the nearest field. The poor lad felt battered and bruised; he needed some rest, *and* a place to hide. His corny horror-movie evening had twisted into this nightmarish night, and he knew that all his troubles had started when he'd taken the bracelet and freed the scarecrow.

'And what was that the beetles said about a Pumpkin King?' Jase wondered just how he could have been so foolish. *'One shouldn't steal things - even in a dream, it seems.'*

He wandered, hungry, weary and dazed ~ so much so, that he failed to notice the grass turning into nettle plants: towering dandelions with jagged petal teeth, then a jungle of jumbled tangled brambles.

'I'd need a flippin' butcher's knife to hack a path through this,' Jase tutted; and he proceeded slowly through the moonlit gloom, between the confusing crisscross stalks.

Suddenly the boy heard a hefty *thump!*

Then a much closer *clomp!*

Behind him another *thump!* (This one made him jump.)

Jase took a step back and, feeling a thorn poke his cloak, he jumped the other way, turning to see that the noises were made by falling fruits ~ giant bulging red berries lying there like mouldy boulders.

'Blurgh!' The huge fruit had a gross musty stench, and Jase was careful to avoid them. He didn't even want to touch them ~ *yuck* ~ never mind walk into one, face-first.

The brambles thistled against his clothes, as Jase plodded on through the thorny jungle, everywhere jaggedy hazardous spikes catching him, scratching him once or thrice. The moist musty atmosphere intensified; a whitish mist wisped over his feet. All was bitterly dank, as Jase shivered his way around the fruits, lost within this mildewed forest, losing all hope of ever getting out alive.

'*Urh!*' Now he felt he was wading through something that stuck to his shoes; Jase lifted his leg to see he'd staggered into a gossamer bed composed of veils of tacky thread. He also noticed more of the webbing up among the bramble thorns, drooping with the bodies of gnats and flies (about half of Jase's size) all drowsily buzzing, half-mummified.

This hideous place appeared to be some sort of larder for enormous spiders, stocked with fresh insect meat.

'*Urgh!*' Jase shuddered. Spiders made his flesh crawl most of all. He looked to get away as quickly as he could, but his feet were caught in the trip-wire webbing. Then, even more alarming, he glimpsed a cluster of shadows closing in, of multi-limbed critters that chattered and snickered as they picked their way through the thorny darkness. In desperation, Jase tore at the sticky web, twisting his feet free, pulling strips of it along with him as he dithered this way, that way, which way, seeing the spidery shapes all around him. There was nowhere to run and, in his panic, Jason took the bracelet from his pocket, held up and jingled the moon-glinting charms.

"Don't - don't - don't you come any closer," he croaked, "or I'll put the Pumpkin King's curse on you!"

His idea worked! The shadowy spiders stayed at bay, hissing at Jase and his talisman bracelet.

So he carried on, jangling the chain, inching away, ever watchful, and, after a while, the brambles withered; the thorny stalks thinned out and, in a clearing, he saw a wooden shack with eerie green light flickering from a window ~ just as in the *Tale of the Blazing Man.*

Jase recalled that the hovel was home to a trio of witchy widow crones, and his common sense told him to *'leg it quick and never come back'* ~

However, Jase guessed that he'd need some magical means of escaping Hexhill; and so, if this shack did indeed belong to three witches, this might be his only chance of finding a way to wake from this nightmare.

Jase approached the shack, and knock-knock-knocked upon its door. He waited there, shivering until, at last ~

Creeak!

The mouldering door groaned open and, in the dim candlelight, he found himself face-to-face with a bulbous-bodied brown arachnid with eight beady eyes, and spindly limbs tipped with clipper-claws.

Brown Widow invited the boy inside to meet her sisters, and an uneasy Jase entered the spiders' webby lair.

He did have the charms which might keep him from harm, so he held the chain tight in his fist. Then Jase ducked through into a room where the other two spidery crones (Black Widow, Red Widow) sat around a cauldron, a welcome-warm wood fire crackling beneath it. The whole place smelled of rotten fruit, and Jase could see that the cauldron contained a slime green cider soup bubbling hot with chunks of bobbing apple.

"See, sisters," Brown Widow hissed. "See what the caterpillar dragged in for *us*, tonight."

The spiders chuckled peckishly, so Jason showed them the bracelet straightaway. *Ssss!* The widows shrank back scared, edging into the cobwebbed corners of the room.

"I won't hurt you," Jase said boldly, "if you promise to help me."

The boy explained his dreamy dilemma, hoping that the arachnid witches could find a way to make him wake, and break the curse of the pumpkin-headed scarecrow.

The trio of widows conversed for a moment, then Brown took up a splintery spoon, turned to the cauldron of cider, and stirred. Red Widow then added some grotty ingredients (chopped up nettles, and fresh fly maggots), while Black Widow muttered a few magic words:

"Apples bloat and maggots grow. Lickety slickety, my black fly.
Worm your way around the pot. Boil, bubble, so soon to die."

Blup! Blup! Blup! The cider simmered, and all three widows peeked into the cauldron, watching the maggots wriggle and writhe among the chunks of fruit.

Jase screwed up his nose as a sickly stink souped up from the stew; sour smoke spun up in threads, forming a pale apple-shaped head with skull-like features, three stalky horns, worm-squirming eyes, and split-peel lips.

"Ah!" Black Widow cooed. "Rise, my harvest phantom, rise! Hear us. Speak with us, Autumn Spirit Apple-Jack!"

The spiders bowed to the head, in deference, and the smoky cider spirit hung in the air, opened its lips and proclaimed to Jase: "In order to wake, and break the curse, you will need the wand of Jack O'Lantern, commonly known as the *Pumpkin King*."

'*Oh, not that flippin' scary scarecrow again,*' thought Jase. "So how do I find this *Jack O'Lantern?*" he asked the apple apparition.

"He will return at midnight to his post. There he will seek to make a sacrifice to the Hallowe'en spirits. When you have the wand, you must use it to destroy the bracelet, reciting these words: *Monarch of the magic mound. Free me now from Hexhill's curse!*" And, with that sputtering utterance, Apple-Jack's smoky face faded away.

The cobwebbed room went silent for a moment, before Red Widow sidled up to Jase. "And now, our price for this advice," she said, brandishing a knife.

The boy certainly hadn't forgotten *that* part of the tale – *They wanted him to pay with an arm and a leg!*

Jase tried another of the bracelet's charms. "Stay back!" he cried, "you horrible spiders!" His hand closed around the silver droplet, and he felt the trinket evaporate – just as the cider in the cauldron bubbled uncontrollably.

Jase backed away as thick white vapours poured up from the top of the pot; ghostly maggots wormed out from the apples; rancid cider started spouting and frothing forth over the brim. The cauldron rolled from side to side, spilling scalding-hot liquid on the squealing widows. The viscous cider gushed around the room, shrivelling the three spiders, boiling them alive.

Jase retreated fast from the shack, smashed his way through the mouldy door, raced out past a nettle patch, through a field of cheatgrass, and kept on going, kept on breathless …

Eventually, he arrived at a farmstead with aphid stables, a cottage, and a large barn. It was the barn that captured his attention: lit up in the dark, and lively with music.

A cat-killing curiosity got the better of the boy, and Jase went up to the cottage for a closer look, sneaking round the back, to the kitchen. He was hungry, starved of party food. *'Perhaps I might find something to eat here.'*

However, as he peered into a window, he was sniffed out quickly by the insects there.

† Chapter VIII †

The Dance of the Carnivorous Mantids

Jason found himself surrounded again, this time by a gang of mantis creatures; but, unlike the crickets, they seemed less like hooligans, and even invited the boy to join them.

"Well come in!" they chirriped. "Supper is about to begin!"

The insects wouldn't take *'no'* for an answer (though Jase was thinking *'No way in hell!'*), and two of the mantids took him by his arms, and ushered him into the sizeable barn where picnic tables and timber benches were arranged around a straw-strewn floor. There were dozens of the creepy creatures there, a whole harvest nest of them. Each had a tall gangly body, clawed folded forelegs, and triangular heads with big bug eyes stuck on the sides.

"So, young sir," one mantid said politely, plonking Jase down upon the nearest bench, "if you would care to take a pew."

(*Pyoo!* was just what Jase was thinking - as something truly nasty was stinking - as if some numbskull cook had burnt the supper.)

The mantid then presented a carapace tray ~ "First a few *horror d'oeuvres* to whet sir's appetite" ~ offering Jase a selection of mushrooms: "Those are *de capi ta mort*," the mantid pointed. "Those be *bolete sataniq*, these ones *chompinyons à la caq-*"

"Er, what's that mean?" Jase asked.

"Death caps, devilled balls, and mushrooms stuffed with manure."

"Urh!" Jase grimaced, "I mean - *Ooo delicious*. It's a shame I'm not hungry."

"Oh don't talk claptrap," the mantid continued. "Now, our specials this evening are slugs and snails; spider legs, bug guts and caterpillar tails. That's what growing boys should feed on."

Mantis cooks, from the cottage kitchen, brought out food for the assembled insects, laying it on the long picnic tables. There was bread spread with cowpat-paté sprinkled with still-twitching half-alive flies; toasted marshfly mallows on skewers; crispy popcorn compound eyes - with everything over-cooked, and giving off a charcoal stink.

"Don't be shy, *tuck in,*" the mantids goaded, shoving more 'un-appetizers' under Jase's nose. (These weren't quite what he'd had in mind when he'd wished for 'party treats'.)

To the insects, though, the revolting foodstuffs were part of a special festive feast. The barn was decorated with fly-wing bunting, illuminated with stripy lamps ~ what Jase first thought to be paper lanterns, were really fatty caterpillars hanging from the roof, lit at the bottoms so their body sacs burned with a writhing oily glow.

All around him, perched on benches, the mantids jabbed and stabbed at their food. Jase noticed that only half of them ate ~ '*The man mantids,*' he presumed, as all the others wore these long straw skirts (dressed as if this autumnal supper was a tropical Hawaiian luau.)

Music came from a couple of players, one mantid tapping at these sauce bottle chimes, while the other circled its forelimbs around the rims of a row of glasses (containing beetles' blood at various levels). The skillful insects produced shimmering slidy whiny sounds, interspersed with a subtle bottle bonging.

All the while, the manly mantids dined on their nauseating *hot queasine,* stuffing their faces, spitting and burping. The female mantids continued to serve them, dishing up pastry, pudding and pie (their strong pongs bringing a tear to the eye). The cooks put out trays of bats' cheese on biscuits; coagulated bug blood tarts; curly fly cakes on cocktail stakes.

Jase had to pretend to eat these 'delicacies', and tried not to wince at their odious odours. He didn't want to upset the mantids, feeling their eerie agreeable manner could turn sour at any moment. *'After all, nothing else in this nightmare had been nice to him.'*

"Try a snail," one mantis hissed. "It's frazzled to a crisp, and served in sizzling slime."

And she plonked a colossal shell in front of the boy: a curly shell with chunks of tail and snail horns swimming in a steaming green sauce.

"*Urk!*" Jase blurghed. "It smells off! And it looks like snot."

"Oh yes, sir, we only serve the runniest snails."

"Er, maybe later," Jase smiled, but he could see that the insects were getting impatient with him.

"You'll try it, and like it, you little brat!" The irritated mantid leant in nastily. "So man up and sup up!"

Jason thought he was going to 'Oo' spew up. Still, with the vicious-looking insects looking on, he made an attempt to pick up the snail shell ~ "Ow! It's flippin' hot!"

Jase dropped it before it scalded his hands, and the shell rolled off the picnic table, spilling a great green splat of slime as ~ *Tish!* ~ it smashed upon the ground.

"Whoops!" Jase shrugged at the livid lady mantid.

"You'll sweep up that mess and eat it!" threatened the insect. "Every last splop!" She stormed off, and came back with a broom, which she thrust into Jase's hands. Then, prodding him painfully, with a claw, told him: "Get to it, maggot!"

"Wish this was a *witch's broomstick*," Jason muttered under his breath. "I'd jump on it and fly away from this dungheap."

"*When we've finished supper,*" he heard the mantis chefs confer, "*we'll make the horrible little brat clean up after us. We could keep him chained up in the kitchen. Yes yes! Force him to do all the chores. Wash the dishes! Sweep the floors! Scrub the tables! Clean the stables!*"

Jason dawdled, pushing the broom across the sickly slick-splattered straw; he could barely shift the bits of broken snail shell, and nearly slipped on the disgusting slime.

In the meantime, the male mantids finished their meals, and the dozens of gargantuan insects congregated upon the floor space. Jason watched from the side of the barn, as the blood-curdling music resumed ~ no longer the lively melody of before, but more a funeral march, with the weird whine of the beetle-juice glasses, and the sombre clang of a spoon on a pan gong.

The mantid males bowed to the females, lining up in tidy rows, nodding their heads and bobbing their bodies, gorged with grub, feeling dozy-doze. The partners paired up, clinging close ~ hips to hips, and heads to heads ~ performing slow stately movements with intricate sets of gangly legs. In fancy patterns, the mantids danced across the floor of the old barn lair ~ till the ladies seized their docile partners, crisscross forelegs folded in prayer. Then Jase stared aghast as the female insects suddenly used their sawlike legs to snap the necks of their mantid mates and, with a few sharp chops, cut off their heads.

The music quickened, each bash of a pan the death knell for another male mantis; yet the decapitated insects kept on hopping in a gruesome wiggle buggy-woogy jitter twitchy-leg jig. Their quick quirky jerky corpses jiggled as in a macabre ballet, eventually collapsing to the barn dance floor, their dizzy feeler-trembling heads still rock 'n' rolling in the straw.

With the pulse of the music livelier again, the females jigged in celebration, arm-in-arm they kicked and twirled, straw skirts whirling with joyful gyration. Finally, they lay their partners' bodies on the tables, gathered up the severed heads ~ and ate.

Jase was nearly sick at the sight of the cannibal mantids chowing down. The females savoured this vile meal. Taking their partners in their jaws, they ate them while they're good and raw; their grotesque, almost mechanical munching, crunching munching, plucking eyes, sucking at the brains and gooey insides.

Jase had already ditched the broom, and started to edge away from the tables. '*Ugh!*' He thought. '*I'm definitely not cleaning up after that!*'

So, while the insects were engrossed in their feasting, Jase took his chance, and snuck out of the barn.

However, he heard a mantis shrieking ~ "Ere! Where's that *brat-worst* gone?" ~ followed by a feverish commotion.

The monstrous mantids set after Jase as he stole away from the rustic place. He ran and ran, crossing a wheat field, trying to lose the insects there.

His terrified heart beating furiously fast, Jase dashed between the head-high blades, wheat stalks whipping past his face.

He could hear the mantids springing after him, slashing their raptor-limbs, cutting a path to him. "Find that brat! Sniff him out! Head him off! He won't get away!"

Suddenly the field ended and, the boy blundered into a patch of giant toadstools, their fat crooked oaken trunks topped with a canopy of shady caps.

Jase had to stop for a second, clutching a stitch that stung his side, queasy, wheezing. *'Where can I hide?'*

But, in moments, he saw the mantids emerge, some of them holding flaming torches. Like an angry mob of horror-movie villagers, they made their way between the toadstools, hunting him, taunting him ~ as though playing some sinister childrens' game. "Come out, come out, wherever you are! We're going to eat you! Tasty or not!"

They giggled girlishly, snapped their mouths, swished their legs with slicing gestures.

"Here comes a mantis to cleave off your head! We'll catch you, snatch you, and chew you up for dead!"

Jase kept moving blindly through the toadstool labyrinth, only just evading the mantids in the dark, glimpsing the insects as their torches flickered past, picking out the hungry gleams in their eyes.

Again, Jase thought he ought to try one of the bracelet charms, and he held the chain in his shivering fist, wished and wished for some means of escape.

This time, the moon-trinket glowed and disappeared, and Jase soon stumbled, from the toadstool patch, into a clearing where he saw, up ahead ~ *There!* ~ a decent place to hide: a seemingly-abandoned wicker basket, big enough to fit inside.

† Chapter IX †

The Attack of the Monster Moths

As Jase got closer to the boxy basket, he saw a weird globe above it beginning to burn like a miniature sun ~ It was the air bag of an air balloon, with a huge candle heating it, inflating it. Jase presumed his charm had worked, to produce this balloon, as if by magic, as a means of evading the chasing mantids. He darted around the side of the basket, to find the rope which tied it to the ground.

"Aaa!" Jase was startled by a giant axe-wielding ant ~ a red-headed ant, standing tall on two hind legs, and wearing a long white scientist's coat (so the insect was more like an ant-headed *man* ~ perhaps the result of some genetic experiment gone horribly wrong).

The ant-man swung its axe. Jase backed away quick ~ *Shuck!* But the ant was only looking to cut the anchor rope, and it jumped aboard the basket as the balloon began to rise.

Jase could see the mantis huntresses scampering from the toadstools towards him, so he tried to clamber into the basket too, using the rope to haul himself up, hanging on for dear life, his vampire cloak flapping behind him. In no time, the balloon was some way off the ground, clear of the torch-bearing mob. Jason desperately scrambled inside ~ to find himself trapped in a basket with a mad man-ant.

"Bug off out my airship!" it cried, grasping the boy's arms with its claws. "The *sugar's* all mine, you mucky crook!"

The ant-man put its face in close ~ its dead red eyes, jagged mandibles, quivering feelers ~ resembling some frightful extraterrestrial.

"I was being chased-" explained Jase, "by ~ Hold on, *what sugar?*"

"*Moon sugar! Moon sugar!*" The ant-man shook him again and again.

Jase broke the insect's grip, then stepped away. "The moon?" he said. "Is that where we're headed?"

"Where *I'm* headed, *stupid!*" the ant replied rudely. "Everyone knows the moon's made of magic sugar. That's why it shines so bright. So, when I get there, and bring back sackloads of it, I'll be rich, won't I?"

"Why are you going in the middle of the night, though?"

"The moon's only there at night, isn't it? You idiot!"

"I'm sure the moon's there all the time," said Jase. "And you'll never get there in an *air balloon.*" (He'd heard of mad scientists, before ~ but this ant was a nutter *lunatic.*)

The insect snorted at the boy's obvious ignorance regarding inter-lunar balloonery. "Need to go higher to break through the sky, don't I?"

And the ant began huffing and puffing at the candle in a crazy attempt to make it burn brighter.

"Don't do that, you'll blow the flame out!"

Jason peered over the side of the basket to see how far up the balloon had taken them.

He was somewhat relieved to see they were only floating high enough to clear the top of a house or tree (although that was still a long way to fall).

As the glowing balloon rose steadily upwards, soon he could see for miles around, over the patchwork matchstack land, fields bright with burning bonfires. Hexhill Common was uncommonly vast, a panoramic world in itself, ringed with an endless flame. If Jase couldn't find the Pumpkin King by midnight, he seemed condemned to remain in this nightmare ~ his only way out some grim demise at the hands and claws or biting maws of the insect hordes. Jason really *was* a jinx ~ to *himself,* in this place.

He squinted at the creatures below: beetle bums assembled round braziers; mobs of grasshopper yobbos on the prowl; another barn full of dancing mantids; a bramble patch of spidery arachnids. Other insects were still at work, an army of them on the ant farms.

"Ugh! Look at all those ants down there!" Jase squirmed. "They look just like people!"

"*Argh*, those ants are cretinous peasants!" fumed the balloonist. "They called *me* insane! Well, look at me now! On the way to the moon! And soon all the sugar in space will be mine!"

Jase ignored the raving ant-man, and scanned the land, believing he recognized a few of the landmarks.

'There!' That had to be the crickets' pitch (now a battlefield piled with insect dead), and *'There!'* a flock of ravens herding aphids, setting bonfires ~ He must be nearly over the field where he'd first seen the scarecrow. *'If only I could take this balloon down now.'*

Despite the heat of the flickering candle, it was cold up high in the wicker airship. Jason shivered. He was beginning to feel light-headed too. "How are we supposed to get down?" he asked the ant-man.

"We don't want to get down. We want to go higher!"

"Look, you'll *never* reach the moon in this balloon," Jase said. "And the higher you go, the less air there is."

"Oh, shut ya face," snapped the bad-tempered ant. "And - I'll never reach the moon with *you* weighing me down!" The ant-man made a lunge at Jase, aiming to throw him overboard. Then it noticed the glinting bracelet poking from his waistcoat pocket. The ant-man snatched it, inspected it ~ *"Aaah! The scarecrow's curse!"*

And Jase could only look on, in despair, as the ant threw the bracelet out of the basket. "No! You stupid rotten loony! Without that chain I can't wake up!"

"Well, you can damn well go after it then!" And the ant attempted to grab him again, roughly pulling the boy by his cloak.

The balloon rocked, the candle guttered, the wicker creaked as the two of them tussled. The four-armed insect wrestled Jase to the edge of the basket, almost pushing him over the side. Yet the boy held on, feeling airsick, peering down on the darkened land.

Wafts of wind suddenly blustered through his hair, and the night seemed to move alive. Shadowy shapes swerved ominously through the sky.

"What the heck's that?" yelled the ant-man.

Jase felt something zip past the basket, and he managed to stick his head back inside - In the nick of time too, as four giant hawk moths fluttered out of the starry darkness, like cross-winged planes soaring ring-a-ring around the balloon. They brushed the air bag, making it wobble, then closed in on the basket itself, clinging to it with quick clawed legs, batting at the air with their blurry brown wings.

Jase recoiled at their thick hairy bodies. The ant, however, seized the airship's candle, and swished it at the massive moths in an attempt to scare them away.

It was the flame, though, that attracted them, and more and more flew up to attack, to claw their way inside the basket, wings *thu-thu-thump*ing against the wickerwork. The ranting ant-man jabbed them with the candle, setting their papery wings alight ~ and soon the balloon was surrounded by moths, some with flickering wings of fire; a few of them plummeted, like blazing comets. Yet still, the howler moths came at them, a virtual lepidopteran squadron swirling, burning, hissing by, zigzag through the blackened sky.

Now, with no fire to heat the balloon, only the hovering moths clinging to the basket, kept it aloft ~ rocking it, jolting it, snatching for the ant-man's candle. Jase felt even more airsick now, his stomach blupping up and down.

"Help me, you idiot!" The ant continued to kick at the moths, and swat them with the candle, singeing their wings, and inadvertantly burning through the ropes that held the balloon.

The basket tipped, allowing one moth to nab the ant, and yank it out antennae-first.

Jason watched in horror as the falling ant-man thrashed through the air ~ only for two huge moths to swoop and tear it limp from lump from limb ~ the lunatic insect dissected in seconds, and scattered across the common below.

Jase was only just hanging on, and with the airship on fire, he was surely a goner.

Suddenly, though, a moth fluttered beneath him. Jase glanced down to see, glittering in the moonlight, the charm bracelet snagged on its body.

Feeling the creeping heat of the fire, he jumped ~ *flumpf!* ~ onto the back of the monstrous beast ~ just as the rest of the moths flapped away, letting the balloon and its fiery basket spiral down and *Crash!* to the ground.

† Chapter X †

The Magic Ring of the Pumpkin King

It was hairy and gross on top of the moth, and Jase could barely see past its wings, or even through the clouds of smoke billowing out from the bonfires below.

Whooshwooshwoosh. They floated closer to the ground, circling the burning stacks which gave off flakes of luminous ash, and leafy licks of fire.

Jase had to cover his face from the flaming maelstrom swirling past the mammoth moth. The shower of fire struck his hands – "Ow ow ow!" – stinging his skin, searing holes in his clothes, a pattern of *smoker-dots* all across him. (His Hallowe'en costume was in terrible nick now, torn and burned, and grubby from his many nightmarish encounters.)

Jase retrieved the charm bracelet, untangling it from the moth's rough hide, worrying how he was going to get down.

He needn't have fret. The moth just dropped him, turning abruptly, tipping the boy ~ *crunch!* ~ onto an unlit haystack. Thankfully, only the hay went *crunch*, and not his poor exhausted bones.

Jase lay there, for a second, in the silence after the monster moth had fluttered off. He made sure the bracelet was safe in his pocket. Now, only one of its charms remained; he wondered if he'd need its magic to obtain the wand from the Pumpkin King.

Jason looked up to the 'sugar-bright' moon.

'Was it midnight now? Would it ever be anything other than midnight here on Hexhill? A never-ending mid-nightmare?'

As he went to get down from the stack of grass, Jase heard something stir around him. *'Urh!'* He was shocked to discover these man-size chrysalis things tucked amongst the hay ~ garish green cocoons, some of them shaking, about to hatch. It must have been the moths' nest, and Jason scrambled from the haystack, almost running into a colossal caterpillar that curled out in front of him, its body lined with poisonous spines.

Then another of the repulsive creatures appeared, coiling loopily up to Jase, its lumpen head with a pincer-maw and lustrous eyelets.

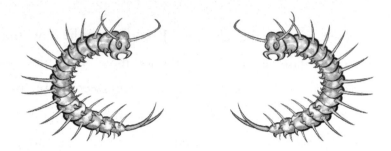

Mercifully, the caterpillars were slow, pulsing along on their knobbly legs, more interested in feeding on hay than bony little boys ~ So Jase dashed past them, into the nearest mass of corn-grass, making his way through, flinching at the slightest noise. Corn stalks brushed him, making him jump. He had butterflies in his stomach, and wondered how that could be: *'I swear I didn't eat any.'*

Jason knew he was near the field where he'd first seen the pumpkin-headed scarecrow. He felt drawn there somehow, pulled by some invisible chain; and he soon found a clearing, the area around the scarecrow's post burnt away, making a large charcoal circle, as if in preparation for some sinister ceremony.

The place had been scary enough, hours earlier, in the light of the late afternoon. Now it was moonlit, vague, misty, and *eerie-mysteery*. Jase would just have to wait here for the Pumpkin King ~ then try to take the wand, destroy the bracelet and break the curse.

As he entered the clearing, Jase thought he saw the scarecrow fastened to its post once more. But, now he looked closer, he could see it was a *different* figure (put there by the raven, perhaps), tied upright by strawy rope to the thick wooden stake. Jase dared to go nearer, treading as softly as he could across the charcoal circle.

The figure was draped in a ragged black dress, its head flopped forward, a mop of hair obscuring its features.

Jase reached up to sweep back the straggly hair, and –

"Aaah!"

He jumped back, as this pale-skinned figure shrieked in his face. It was his sister Felicity.

"*Fifi?* What in *hell* are you doing here?"

"*Jinx?* Ah, I might have known *you'd* turn up in my nightmare!"

"It isn't *your* nightmare," Jase said. "It's *mine.*"

"What the *blazes* you on about? I – I must have dozed off or something – cuz I woke up on this flaming common, tied to this post." Felicity tried to shift the rope twined around her ankles and wrists. "Come on then, *Jinx*, flippin' help-" She suddenly stared past him. "*Hide, Jinx, quick,*" she uttered in a low scared voice. "Something's coming! Something evil, I can *feel it –*"

Jase peeked round. Someone *was* approaching. He could see these far-off fiery eyes.

"Just scram, Jinx!" Felicity hissed.

Jase did as she said, and he scampered away to hide in the grass surrounding the circle.

Jack O'Lantern stepped into the clearing, stalking slowly up to the pole. Earlier, Jase had found the scarecrow merely startling, but now he'd transformed into this menacing spectre, no longer in tatty cast-off clothes, but wearing robes of shimmering velvet - fit for the Pumpkin King of Hallowe'en.

"Harh!" grinned the orange-headed fiend, strutting around the scarecrow's pole, scrutinizing Jase's terrified sister. "See what someone's nightmare brought into my magic ring! Isn't the power of wish-filled thinking, of dreaming and fear, a wonderful thing?"

Jack O'Lantern twirled extravagantly, and with summoning gestures - *puh puh puh* - a whole ring of pumpkins blew-bloomed, growing out of the grey dead ground; ghoulish heads with eyes aglow, mocking grins and candle tongues.

"Meet my scare-cronies!" Jack proclaimed. "Tonight, they rise from the soil, to feast!"

Felicity began to weep, as the fire-fanged spectre gripped her hair, and forced her head back. The heat from his flaming mouth burned her cheek.

"Well, *witch*, you owe your situation to the fool who freed me from my curse. Your own *little brother*," Jack O'Lantern snarled, "who stole the charm that damned me to remain here, tethered to this scarecrow's pole. But now the spell is broken, and I'm free to feed you to my pumpkin-men." Jack squeezed Felicity's face with his twiggy fingers. "Mmm, a choice sacrifice. For one night only - *Hah, witch! You'll be Queen of All Hallowe'en!*"

At these words, Jack plucked a pumpkin from the ring of grinning heads. He cracked its skull-like husk in half, and positioned one of the jagged pieces as a crown upon Felicity's brow. Then he pressed a sceptre into her hand, a wooden stick tipped with a pentacle star.

'The Pumpkin King's wand!' Jase thought, as he spied. *'That's what I need - to get out of here alive!'*

† Chapter XI †

The Burning of the Witch

"Now then," Jack O'Lantern uttered to Felicity, "let's set you alight! We'll feast on roasted witch, this night!"

Felicity's eyes widened as Jack took the candle from the broken pumpkin, and held it there in front of her face, scorching the fringe of hair at her forehead. Next, he set fire to the hem of her dress.

Jase had to think quick. *'The bracelet! The final charm!'*

The only trinket left on the chain was the cat of black volcanic glass. And, all the while that Jack had been speaking, Jase had been holding onto the bracelet, wishing for vital magical help. However, nothing was happening. He had to take a risk himself.

Jason sprinted across the clearing, and leapt over the ring of ghoulish fruit. He surprised the Pumpkin King, shoved him to the ground. Then he patted at Felicity's clothes, hurting his hands, putting the flames out, before ripping at the ropes that bound her to the pole.

Felicity kicked and wrenched herself free, threw down the wand, and turned to flee ~

By now, though, Jack was back on his feet, cackling maniacally; and the pumpkin-men, surrounding them, began to climb from the charcoal soil.

Jase made sure he picked up the wand; then he clutched Felicity by the arm, and together they dared to nip past the pumpkins, evading their grasping leafy limbs, making it into the moonlit field, dashing through the corn stalks as fast as they could.

After a while, all went quiet. It seemed they'd gotten away, and the two of them stopped to catch their breaths.

"So, what's this about a - a *charm* you stole, Jinx?"

Jase showed Felicity the bracelet chain. "It's supposed to protect against evil, I think. I've just got to use the wand to destroy it. Then I'll wake up - and we'll both be out of this nightmare, okay?"

Jase lay the bracelet down on the ground, took the sceptre, pointed, and recited (Apple-Jack's words had burned in his mind): *"Monarch of the magic mound. Free me now from Hexhill's curse!"*

Nothing happened.

"Well?" said Felicity.

"Nothing happened," Jason uttered.

"I can see nothing's happened, *Count Thickula*."

"But I don't understand. I'm supposed to wake up now."

Jase pointed the wand again. (He even tapped its star at the chain.) He said the magic words and - again, nothing happened.

"Free me *now!*" he repeated, frustrated. *"Free me now from Hexhill's curse! Free me from this flippin' curse!"* Jase fell to his knees, in despair. "It didn't work," he wept. "Stupid mouldy apple lied to me! I'll be stuck here forever."

Felicity knelt beside her brother. She took the wand from his trembling hand. "It's just a piece of wood, Jinx. Of course it doesn't work. It *isn't* magical."

"But it must be," the boy mumbled. "The apple in the spider's cauldron said so-"

"Apple?" said Felicity. *"Spider's cauldron?* What are you on about?"

"It was a *talking* apple," Jase explained, "made of magic maggot smoke -"

"Listen to yourself, Jinx! You're probably in shock. You're ranting like a nutbag! If this is a nightmare ~ then all you have to do is *cruddy well wake up!*" Felicity slapped him twice across his face.

"Ow!" said Jase. *"Ow!* Stop hitting me. That never works!" And he tried to describe the dream-logic to her - how he can only wake up after solving some problem or achieving some specific goal. "My mind usually conjures up something to help me. In *this* nightmare, I guess it's *you-*"

"Is that why that *pumpkin-git* kept calling me a *witch?*" squeaked Felicity. "Is that how you really think of me, *Jinx?*"

"Er -"

"In *your* mind, I'm a mean old witch? You really *are* a *spiteful* little step*bother* - Hah! Little Bother Jason Jinx! *Ha har, haha har!*" Felicity gave a loud scratchy cackle, which made Jase shrink away. She suddenly realized how she must have sounded. "Oh, Jinx - I mean, Jason - *Jase*, I'm so sorry. I don't know what came over me. It's this freaky spooky place -"

"Yeah, I know," said Jase. "I - I'm sorry too. But if that wand doesn't work, we'd better get the hell out of here!"

Felicity picked up the bracelet, and slipped it round her wrist; then she jabbed Jase with the star-tipped sceptre, (*"Ow!"*) urging him to his feet.

The two of them stumbled on through the dark, and it wasn't long before the cornfield cleared ~

They found themselves back at the charcoal circle, with Jack O'Lantern waiting, laughing.

"Foolish witch! Stupid fool! We'll eat you *both* alive!" he cried. "You can't escape this magical place!"

95

At the Pumpkin King's words, the earth began to quake. The charcoal circle swelled into a mound, rising, rising from the ground ~ a true *Hex-hill*, from which the troop of pumpkin-men creepily grew.

Jack floated phantomly towards his victims, eyes blazing, spitting fire. He grabbed for Felicity and Jase with his branching arms. The two of them ducked, and called out together: *"Leave us alone, you flaming pumpkin!"*

A fiery light suddenly flared above the cornfield.

Fhwoo! Fhwoo! Fhwoo!

Jack and his scare-cronies stared about as raging flames encircled the hill, a fluttering ring of butterfly-fire, gradually forming a jagged figure. Jase could feel the increasing heat. The figure flickered, bright then black, a silhouette in the shape of a cat ~ or rather some feline demon creature, with fiery tiger's eyes and fangs.

The pumpkin cronies wailed in terror and, before they could scarper, the cat-demon swiped its tail, setting fire to each in turn. Their stalky limbs began to quiver, fizzing as fuses, sprackling like sparklers, shrivelling up at the demon's touch. Then the cat extended it claws, plucked their lumpy heads, and juggled the pumpkins, eventually consuming them, one by one, the earthly fiends going up in smoke.

Felicity and Jase just cowered as fire flowered all around them. The black cat demon roared and hissed; its flaming screams tore into the night sky, all the way to the sugary moon.

Jack O'Lantern froze in fear as the demon reached down with outstretched claws, crumpled the Pumpkin King up in its paws, and dropped him ~ *Crrunch!* ~ upon the mound. Jack became a pitiful scarecrow once more, in frazzled clothes, with a charred dead pumpkin head *sissling* out a squeamy steam.

Jase and his stepsister blinked in awe as the blazing cat then simply vanished, fizzling into the starry ether.

All fell silent on the charcoal mound. Felicity knelt to look at the scarecrow lying there amidst the ashes of his pumpkin-men.

"Owh!" She jumped back in shock, as a blackened hand grasped her wrist, trying to seize the glistening bracelet. Jack's carved eyes still glowed. Felicity broke his hold, and kicked the scarecrow away in disgust.

Jack O'Lantern coughed and laughed, managing to rasp out a last dying curse: "Whatever you sow, shall you reap!" he vowed. "The charms of the bracelet will return to haunt you, and torture you a hundredfold!"

The scarecrow crumbled, and his head deflated farty flat like the fetid rooty fruit it was.

"What did he mean, Jase?" asked Felicity. "What have you been doing with this bracelet?"

† Chapter XII †

The Gathering of the Undead Hordes

Jason felt a shiver up his spine hearing a rustling, twittering trilling, softly at first, then steadily louder. Sounds from the surrounding field. All around the charcoal mound, limbs and feelers, then heads appeared, the undead bodies of giant insects sprouting out of the enchanted earth.

"What the *heck* did you *do* with this bracelet, Jase?"

"Er," he uttered, "I may have - *accidentally* squished a few bugs."

"A few? There's *bloody hundreds* of them!"

Hordes of bugs, of roasted beetles, mangled mantids, fried spiders ~ all of those, that had perished on this nightmare night, were back to wreak their vengeance on *Jason Jinx*, to punish him for his accursed wishes.

Spitten crickets, chopped-up butterflies, slaughtered weevils joined the ranks ~ swarms of desiccated corpses stirring, rising in the bright moonlight.

Grasshoppers and ants were also conjured from the Hexhill soil, their heads popping up above the corn crop, looking as though they'd been created by the maddest of mad scientists.

The festering creatures ascended the mound (some of them partly-decomposed, with dripping eyes, blistered skins, limbless stumps and open wounds), drawing nearer to Jase and his sister who retreated, in horror, at the putrescent stench.

Now though, the star on Felicity's wand began to glow. She felt a bewitching tingle of energy ripple through the bracelet too. Her black dress turned shiny and golden. (Even her stepbrother's vampire costume was restored to its pristine *Draculaic* glory.)

"You really do have witchy powers!" Jase exclaimed. "Quick, Fifi! Use the wand! Think of a spell to get rid of the bugs!"

Felicity turned to the insect abominations clawing their way up the slope of the hill. She pointed her wand, and concentrated. The star emitted a flash of light. It struck one of the massive crickets which burst with a violent *splurt*, instantly rotting into dust.

"You *did* it, Fiifs!" grimaced Jase. "Now try it again - a few hundred times!"

Felicity zapped a couple more bugs. Then, growing in confidence, she wielded the wand with wild slashing gestures, cutting down dozens and dozens at a time. The insects exploded with green splats of guts, spraying slimy blood and pus.

The creeping crawlers kept on coming. The crawling creepies kept on going, blowing up at the zaps from the wand. Felicity smirked naughtily as she detonated the waves of insects.

Jase just stood and squinted, wincing - thinking how his sister seemed to be enjoying the massacre a bit too much. She even began to do fancy dance twirls, pointing and zapping. More bugs went splatting.

(*'Perhaps I ought,'* Jase now thought, *'to be a hell of a lot nicer to Fifi in future.'*)

However, from the top of the hill, the boy could see more undead creatures, never-ending hordes of them diminishing into the distant darkness: bloodthirsty beetles, vicious crickets, carnivorous mantids, arachnids and ants; so many rising, multiplying, their massed chirruping chirruping chirruping making a shrill, almost deafening cacophony.

From the sky too, a squadron of ravens and hawk moths cluttered the air, zeroing in on the mound. Felicity could never 'shoot' them all down.

Jason wondered how he could help.

He shuddered at the sight of the twitchy-legged bugs ascending from the field all around.

Then he realized –

"Fifi!" he cried. "*You're* the Queen of Hallowe'en!"

"That's very flattering, Jase," she replied, zapping a beetle right between its eyes. "But not very helpful–"

"No! I mean, *you're* now the *monarch of the magic mound!* We have to try the spell with the bracelet again! Fifi, quick! Before it's too late!"

Felicity stopped her zombie-zapping, took off the bracelet, put it on the ground, and pointed the wand. "This better work, Jinx, or we've had it!"

"It didn't work before because we needed to be *here*, in the charcoal circle. And with the Pumpkin King defeated, you took his place -"

The swarm of undead insects closed in.

"Don't explain, Jinx! Just say the *bloody magic words!*"

Again Jase recited the spell: *"Monarch of the magic mound. Free me now from Hexhill's curse! Free me now from Hexhill's curse!"*

Vroosh! The wand burned up in his sister's hand.

Zap! The bracelet vanished in a fiery flash ~

He got out of the car, and yawned, baring his fake Dracula fangs.

A black cat was sitting on the garden wall of his mate's house. Felicity went over to stroke it.

The cat purred for her, but it hissed at Jase.

"*Ha,*" teased Felicity. "This cat doesn't like you. It's got good taste."

"*Har har,* Fiif. You're still *really* funny."

"Perhaps I'll ask Mom and Dad if *we* can get a pet cat. I'll name it Jinxy - after *you.*"

And so Felicity left Jase to his party.

"Don't get too frightened by the scary-wary movies!" she called. "I'll be back in the morning to rescue you. I'll bring you a change of underwear too, in case you wet yourself!" Felicity got in her car, cackling with laughter, and Jase watched her drive away, hoping no one had heard her.

Walking up to his mate's house - *Hiss!*

"Oo, that flippin' cat!" made Jase jump.

Then he saw that someone had put a jack-o'-lantern pumpkin on the ground, by the front door. Candlelight shone from its carved skull features: the slanted evil eyes, the hole in its nose, and the jagged teeth in its great grinning mouth.

"*Huh,*" Jason Rascal muttered. "I've had enough of *cruddy pumpkins.*"

And he kicked the jack-o'-lantern hard, booted it right in its grinning mush.

It rolled away across his friend's front lawn, spitting flames across the grass ~ till *Crack!* it broke against the garden wall, and the flame of the pumpkin sputtered and died.

The first season …

Jason Rascal's SPRING iN TiME

On a spring day out to Strudel Wood, a dozy Jase idly wanders through a dream-gate ~ and enters a world of extinct beasts: mossy rhinoceroses, sabertooth tigers, mastodons, and weird wooden dinosaurs that seem to grow from the trees around him…

It's Jase against Time!

Helped by Stumpy, a grumpy giant tortoise, Jase must escape the perilous prehistoric past, and find his way back to present day reality ~ before he himself becomes extinct!

Last season ...

Jason Rascal's
MAD
SUMMER
GAMES

One sunny summer day at the seaside, Jase dozes off whilst playing a computer game ~ only to wake in a virtual desert world where he is met by the Inter-Newt, a sandy salamander who gives him a series of sporting trials: eight strange games to complete before the sun runs out of power.

Jase has to race in a millipede truck ... fight spidery Sand Invaders armed only with a frisbee ... play crazy golf against four giant scorpions ... help a team of seagulls win at soccer ... go surfing the ocean on a crocodile board ... compete with lobsters at octopus-tennis ... be a life-sized pinball chased by ghosts ...

And, as if the trials weren't tricky enough, his desert world has been infiltrated by a destructive snaky mutating bug!

Can Jase even make it to the last crazy game ~
or will his life be (bli-blip) Game Over?

About the author

Neale Osborne was born in 1970, in Birmingham, England.
A freelance illustrator since 1992,
his pictures of various beauties and beasties
have appeared in a wide variety of places:
in books and programmes, on posters and websites,
(even sweet packaging, plates and teapots);
and in such publications as the *Gramophone*, *Mojo*,
Country Life, the *Mail* and the *Times*.

His debut children's novel *'Lydia's Tin Lid Drum'*
~ published by Oxford University Press in 2009 ~
is an epic fantasy adventure set on *Planet Plenti*,
a world full of magical sweet-themed lands.

It was followed, in 2013, by *'Lydia's Golden Drum'*
a stand-alone sequel with the spicy flavour
of the *Arabian Nights*.